"An excellent collection to read aloud or for older children to read themselves." *Scotland on Sunday*

Sam McBratney was a teacher for many years and is now a full-time writer. Twice winner of the Bisto Children's Book Award, he has written many books, stories and radio plays for adults and children, including the classic picture book *Guess How Much I Love You*. Among his other books are *The Dark at the Top of the Stairs*; *Just You and Me*; *Art, You're Magic!*; *Flash Eddie and the Big Bad Wolf*; *Oliver Sundew, Tooth Fairy*; *Kristel Dimond, Time Cop* and *In Crack Willow Wood*. Married with three grown-up children and an ancient tortoise, he lives in County Antrim, Northern Ireland.

Also by Sam McBratney

Bert's
Wonderful News

Written by
SAM MCBRATNEY

Illustrated by
BRITA GRANSTRÖM

WALKER BOOKS
AND SUBSIDIARIES
LONDON • BOSTON • SYDNEY

First published 1998 by Walker Books Ltd
87 Vauxhall Walk, London SE11 5HJ

This edition published 1999

2 4 6 8 10 9 7 5 3

Text © 1998 Sam McBratney
Illustrations © 1998 Brita Granström

The right of Sam McBratney to be identified as author of this
work has been asserted by him in accordance with the
Copyright, Designs and Patents Act 1988.

This book has been typeset in Plantin Light.

Printed in England by Clays Ltd, St Ives plc

British Library Cataloguing in Publication Data
A catalogue record for this book is
available from the British Library.

ISBN 0-7445-6396-8

CONTENTS

"I've got a plaster and you haven't,"
said Geraldine Greer.

PLASTERS

Geraldine Greer from next door came into Bert's garden wearing a pink plaster on her knee. Bert wished that he had one, too. He quite liked wearing plasters.

"I've got a plaster on my sore leg and you haven't," said Geraldine Greer.

"I don't care," said Bert, although actually, he did care – this was a big and important looking plaster.

"Ha haa, I bet you do care," laughed Geraldine.

The sound of Geraldine Greer's giggling face laughing at him in his own garden didn't please Bert at all.

"You haven't really got a cut," he said. "It's probably only pretend."

"Yes I have got a cut, I fell on glass at the beach and there was blood everywhere but I'm not taking the plaster off my sore leg just to show you!" cried Geraldine.

As soon as Geraldine Greer went home, Bert marched into his own house.

"Daddy, can I have a plaster for my leg, please?" he said.

"What for?"

"Geraldine Greer has one on her knee."

"Well, she must have a cut on her knee," said his dad. "She needs a plaster to keep the dirt out of her cut, that's what they're for. Come and help me with lunch. Liz is coming round to see us."

Good, thought Bert. Liz was a friend of his daddy's who sometimes gave Bert squashy hugs and called him "Sugar".

After lunch, an awful thing happened. A wasp sneaked in through Bert's window and stung Liz on the arm. All of a sudden she said "Yeow!", and soon there was a red mark where the wasp had jabbed her with its stinger.

"Is it sore?" asked Bert.

"Oooh well, it's a bit sore," said Liz.

When Bert went out to play again, he saw a wasp buzzing round his bin. That cheeky wasp! It had no business coming into his house and stinging Liz like that. Boy, it would be good to zap that wasp, he was thinking as he picked up a big stick. This stick felt like a good thing for zapping wasps.

"Zap!" cried Bert, swinging wildly with the stick. "Zap, wap, zap!"

But the wasp didn't want to be zapped, and it wouldn't be still. It flew close to his ears with a loud bzzzz. Then it landed on his bare leg, and stung him. When Bert ran into his house, he was howling as loudly as he could howl.

"Daddy, Daddy, I was zapping the wasp and it stung me on my leg."

"Oh dear dear, these things happen," said his dad as he sprayed some cold stuff on the sting to take the pain away. He also told Bert that he shouldn't have been zapping the wasps. "You only make them angry. They don't really want to sting people, you know, but they will if you make them angry."

"Do you think I should be the Friend of the Wasps?" asked Bert.

"Yes, you should. Well – not too friendly. Just leave them alone."

"And do you think I need a plaster to keep the dirt out of my sore leg?"

"Good idea," said his dad.

Bert put a plaster on his sore leg. Then he

put a plaster on his other leg where there seemed to be a little bruise. And he put a plaster on his cheek because it felt itchy.

When Bert went outside, he seemed to have plasters everywhere. His friends Meg and Charlie were playing a game with Geraldine Greer.

"What happened to you?" cried Meg.

"I got stung by a wasp and I have to wear plasters," said Bert.

Geraldine Greer, who was only wearing one plaster, didn't say anything.

"Watch this," Bert said, and stepped
right in with both feet.

WELLOW YELLIES

Bert's dad took him into town the next day to buy wellington boots.

Bert had a problem when he got to the shoe shop: which boots should he choose – the red ones or the yellow ones? He liked the red wellies, but it was more fun saying "yellow wellies" than saying "red wellies".

"Make up your mind, Bert," said the shopkeeper. "Do you want the red wellies or the wellow yellies? I mean the yellie wellows. I mean the … Ooo! Now you've got me all mixed up."

"Yellow wellies, please," said Bert.

The sun was shining when Bert went out

with his new boots on. They felt good on his feet – probably the best boots his feet had ever owned. Meg and Charlie and Geraldine Greer saw him coming.

"I've got new wellies," said Bert. "Yellow wellies. I'm looking for a puddle."

"Yellow wellies," said Meg, staring down at his feet. "I'd love a pair of yellie wellies. I mean wellie yellows. I mean…" Meg gave up. "It's not very easy to say those two words, you know."

"Yes it is," said Geraldine. "Yellow wellies, yellow wellies, yellow wellies, yellow wellies, yellow wellows, wellow yellows, yellie yellies…"

As soon as he heard "yellie yellies", Charlie started to laugh.

"Let's hear how good *you* are at saying it!" cried Geraldine; but Charlie shook his head.

"I know where there's a puddle," he said.

"But it's deep."

Bert didn't mind. His boots were for walking in deep puddles and not shallow ones. "Bring me to the puddle," he said.

It wasn't long before they found Charlie's puddle at the bottom of a ditch. It lay there like a long mirror reflecting the sky and the tops of some trees.

"Look how lovely and smooth it is," said Meg. "Like a new plate. It seems a pity to break it."

Bert had not come to admire the puddle, he had come to walk in it.

"Watch this," he said, and stepped right in with both feet. The puddle had a soft, slippery bottom – more than half of his yellow wellies disappeared under the water, which quickly turned muddy. What clever person had thought up wellington boots? Bert suddenly wondered. "Go in a bit further," said Geraldine. "I bet it's not very deep."

"It *is* deep," said Charlie.

Leading with his left foot, Bert took another step, and the cold water slurped over the top of his boot, filling it completely. His sock, his ankle, the boot, and all five of his toes were now under the muddy water.

"I told you it was deep," said Charlie.

Bert got out of there quickly, but far too late, of course. His left foot squelched. The puddle had won.

"Look what you made me DO!" he said angrily to Geraldine Greer. Meg wondered what Bert's daddy would say about this.

Mr Green was not pleased when Bert walked through the door a few minutes later with his left foot squelching. Liz was there, too. Her eyebrows went up as she saw the wet marks across the kitchen floor.

"For goodness sake, Bert," said his dad, "those wellingtons were supposed to keep your feet dry! What is the point of me buying you new boots to keep your feet dry if you are going to get your feet wet? How could you be so silly?"

"Daddy, it was Geraldine Greer's fault. She said it wasn't deep."

"It wasn't Geraldine wearing the wellies," said his dad.

"But I only wet one foot."

Liz held up his left boot and the last of the water slowly dribbled out of it. "That is one wet wellow yellie," she said.

"A wet *what*?" said Bert's dad.

"A wet wellie yellow. I mean a wet yellie wellow. I mean a…"

Liz looked at Bert, Bert looked at his dad, and they all began to laugh.

Goody, thought Bert, a wet foot wasn't so

They all began to laugh.

serious. But the next time I buy boots I'm buying the red wellies and not the yellow ones.

"Are those dead people?" Bert asked.

LOST

I never have News, Bert thought to himself as he came home from school one day. Nothing ever happens to me. Everything happens to somebody else.

He was thinking of his friend Charlie, who got a bead stuck up his nose and had to go to hospital. *That* was interesting News. And he was thinking of his friend Meg, whose photo was in the paper because her dog won a competition.

"I never have News to tell people," Bert said to his daddy when he got home. "Nothing interesting ever happens to me."

His dad hurried Bert into his coat and

didn't seem to care that he never had News. "Come on, let's get to the shops before they close," he said. "I want to look at washing machines."

On the way to town they looked into the windows of many shops. One big shop had lovely low windows for looking through. There were four funny people in the window. Not one of them moved. Two of the funny people were completely bald and one of them had no clothes on anywhere – no trousers, no skirt, no shoes, nothing!

And they didn't blink their eyes even once.

"Daddy?"

"Hmm."

"Are those dead people?"

"Don't be silly, Bert, they're plastic dummies. The shop people dress them up to sell clothes."

Then Bert spotted something even more

interesting. He saw roundy-round doors!

Bert knew all about roundy-round doors – they were his favourite doors. They didn't open, they just turned round and round in circles. You walked into them and kept on walking and you ended up on the pavement again. They turned you right round, like magic!

Bert let go of his daddy's hand and jumped into the doors with both feet. First he went right round once and ended up where he started. Then he went halfway round and stepped into a shop.

He found himself walking down the lanes of one of those big stores that seem to sell everything that anybody might need. Bert counted six lawnmowers like his daddy's and twelve garden spades before there was a sudden change and he was surrounded by high shelves full of TVs and videos.

At the bottom of the moving stairs, where they sold nice smells like Liz sometimes wore, Bert remembered that he wasn't supposed to be on his own. His daddy was supposed to be with him.

But where were the roundy-round doors? Were they in front of him? Or behind? He didn't know! Bert turned round and round in useless circles, for he could see no further than a wall of toothbrushes and shampoos. People passed him by, but they didn't know him, they didn't know that he was Bert.

I am LOST, he thought. Nobody knows where I am.

Once their teacher had read them a story about a girl who got lost in an airport, and now Bert felt that scary feeling, too. He stared around him through big wobbly tears and sucked his top lip in despair.

How long did it last? How long could you

I am LOST, he thought.

be lost for? Would his daddy go home without him?

"Bert! Bert Green, stay where you are!"

A loud voice shouted his name from a long way off. His daddy loomed up in front of him and grabbed him by the arm.

"I have been looking everywhere for you! How dare you disappear like that, you'll have me round the bend one of these days you absolute noodle-head."

Bert sniffed loudly. For once he was happy to be called a noodle-head.

His daddy hadn't finished talking. "Look at you standing there with the tears tripping you. Well it's your own stupid fault for running through those doors like a rabbit down a hole!" Then he gathered him up and gave him a great big squasher of a hug. It felt wonderful not to be lost any more.

On the way home Bert began to think.

Had Charlie or Meg or Geraldine Greer ever been LOST in a great big shop with moving stairs and nice smells – a place where nobody even knew their names?

Probably not. I'll be able to tell them what it's like, thought Bert. *I'll* be the one with the interesting News tomorrow.

Just after lunch Geraldine's tooth came out.

A MISSING TOOTH

Bert loved Miss King, his teacher in school. She taught him how to do numberwork and how to do good writing that wasn't all squashed up. Miss King looked a lot like his daddy's friend Liz.

On Friday morning he tried to tell her his News, but a loud voice piped up first. It belonged to Geraldine Greer.

"Miss King, Bert got lost at the shops yesterday and he was crying. His daddy told my mummy all about it."

Bert was so angry that he could hardly speak. Geraldine Greer wasn't even telling her own news, she was telling his!

"I'm sure that was awful, Bert," said Miss King. "Now let's get our books out or we'll never finish anything today."

They started to work. Bert didn't get time to tell everybody what it felt like to be LOST.

Geraldine Greer had come to school that morning with a wobbly tooth in her mouth. She made it go wibble-wobble with the tip of her tongue until there was blood all over her teeth. Bert could hardly bear to watch her. He didn't like looking at other people's blood.

"How do you like my tooth?" Geraldine said to him on the way up to the hall for PE. "I have to bring it home when it comes out because my mummy keeps all my teeth."

"I don't like it," said Bert, "and stop showing me your blood."

"I will if I want to," said Geraldine Greer.

Every time Bert looked at Geraldine Greer, she wiggled her tooth at him. It happened during play-time and it happened twice during reading. When she did it *again* during numberwork and made him do mistakes, Bert said, "You stop showing me your blood."

"It's my tooth, Bert Green, I can do what I want."

"I'll put my schoolbag over your HEAD."

"Miss King, he says he's going to put his schoolbag over my head!" wailed Geraldine Greer – and a cross voice spoke from the front of the room.

"Bert, I am watching you. Isn't it your turn to feed our fish today at home time?"

Bert glanced at the tank of goldfish near the door. Feeding the fish was one of his favourite things. "It's my turn and Charlie's, Miss King."

"Then be good."

Just after lunch Geraldine's tooth came out and Bert was pleased about this because she couldn't wobble it about any more – but then she opened her lips and made him look at the horrible hole where it used to be. She left the tooth sitting on the table where everybody could see it. One end of it was still red.

Miss King wrote a good poem on the board and the whole class said it together.

"I looked in the mirror
and what did I see?
I saw nothing at all
where my tooth used to be.
When you see me you'll think
that my smile has a space,
But soon a new tooth
will grow in its place."

By now it was nearly home time. As they were tidying up, Charlie said something amazing.

"Miss King, Geraldine's tooth's at the bottom of the fish tank."

It was true. That tooth lay on the gravel at the bottom of the tank like a pearl! The five golden fish swimming round in circles didn't give it a second glance, but Geraldine Greer took one look, then opened her mouth to let the noise come out.

"AAAAA! Those fish have got my tooth! And I have to bring it home with me. My Mummy keeps all my TEETH. AAAAAA!"

Meg and Charlie, who were standing beside her, covered up their ears.

"That's enough, Geraldine," said Miss King as she reached into the tank. "Here, put it in your pocket and stop that noise. Charlie – how did you know the tooth was in that tank?"

"Bert told me," said Charlie.

"Bert – did you put that tooth in with the fish?"

Bert sucked his top lip and didn't say anything, but everyone could tell that he was the guilty one. At last he nodded.

"She was showing me her blood."

"She was, Miss King," said Bert's friend Meg. "She wobbled her tooth at us all the time even when we told her to stop, but she wouldn't stop."

"That is no excuse," said Miss King. "You have to learn to leave other people's things alone. I'm afraid you'll just have to feed the fish by yourself this Friday, Charlie. And let's hope this teaches Bert a lesson."

Bert was far from happy as he walked home that day. He didn't like school any more. Yet again Geraldine Greer had got him into trouble and he wished he had a rubber to rub out Geraldine Greer and make her disappear completely! He'd missed his turn to feed the fish because of her.

Then he had another thought. Maybe Charlie didn't give those fish enough food to eat for Saturday and Sunday. Two whole days. "It won't be my fault if they're dead on Monday," he said to himself. "Everybody's going to be SORRY!"

Geraldine knocked the golden crown off Bert's head.

SAUSAGES AND KINGS

On Saturday morning Charlie and Meg and Geraldine Greer came to Bert's door. Geraldine asked Bert if he wanted to play in her playhouse.

"Yes I do," said Bert, "but we're getting a new washing machine and I want to be here when the lorry brings it."

"We want to play now and we can't wait all day for lorries to come," said Geraldine.

"And the lorry mightn't bring your washing machine until the driver has his lunch," Charlie pointed out.

"All right, I'll come," said Bert.

He didn't actually like Geraldine Greer

very much, but he liked her playhouse. It had a dressing-up box and a red phone and a small cooker. Bert liked to pretend that he was frying sausages on the small cooker.

When they all got down there, Geraldine decided that it would be a good idea to play weddings today.

"I know all about weddings," she said, "I was a flower-girl at my Aunty Jean's wedding and I'm going to marry you, Bert."

"You're not marrying me," said Bert.

"Yes I am, it's my playhouse."

"You're not," said Bert, holding out a handful of little sticks. These sticks were his pretend sausages, the ones he was going to fry on the cooker. "I'm here to cook these sausages."

"You're not! You have to do what I say!" cried Geraldine Greer, angrily stamping her foot on the ground.

Bert stared at Geraldine Greer, wondering what to do about this. If only I could turn into a giant, he thought, I would stamp my foot and make the whole house shake.

"I AM HERE TO COOK THESE SAUSAGES!" he roared.

"It's my COOKER," Geraldine roared, just as loudly.

There was a tapping noise in the kitchen. "I hope you people aren't going to fight in there," Geraldine's mum called out.

Then Bert had a clever idea. There was a crown in the dressing-up box, the sort that Kings wear to make them important. Bert quickly put this crown on his head.

"I'm the King," he said, "and Kings can cook sausages if they want to."

"That's true," said Meg. "Kings can do whatever they like."

"They can't do what they like in my

PLAYHOUSE," cried Geraldine, who suddenly began to screech the way she sometimes did in school when people didn't obey her orders. And she knocked the golden crown off Bert's head.

"You leave my crown alone or I'll zap you," said Bert.

"Mummeee! Bert Green says he's going to zap me in my own playhouse."

Those two made so much noise that Charlie – who didn't like trouble – decided to go home. Mrs Greer arrived clapping her hands. "I'm not having this noise," she said. "Come out of that playhouse this minute my girl, and stop that screeching. And you will have to go back to your own house, Bert Green, until you learn to play properly."

As Bert went back to his own house he was very sure of one thing: he would never ever play with Geraldine Greer again for the rest of his life.

"You're looking very grumpy," said his dad as he walked through the door. "What's the matter with you?"

"Nothing," said Bert, who was thinking that if Geraldine Greer went to live in somebody else's street he would be really happy. Then he saw something that made him forget all about Geraldine Greer.

A cardboard box. A huge cardboard box. Until this moment, Bert did not know that they made cardboard boxes as big as that one.

"Where did it come from?" he said.

"With the new washing machine," said his dad. "The washing machine was inside the box. Come and see. I think Liz is going to like it."

It was a lovely machine, completely new all over and as shiny white as could be. But it wasn't nearly as good as the box.

"Can I have it?" asked Bert.

"I suppose so. What are you going to do with an empty box?"

Bert knew exactly what he was going to do with the box. He turned it on its side and made the flappy bits into doors. He made a little window in the back to look out of, and even made a hole in the roof for a chimney. And when he had finished that he got a black marker and drew lines as if the whole thing was made out of bricks.

"Daddy, come and see, I've made a playhouse!"

His dad was amazed. "What a smasher. It's even got a window," he said.

"And doors! I'll be back in a minute."

Bert ran out to find Meg and Charlie, because he knew they would want to come and try his new playhouse, and maybe even cook sausages.

*Bert knew exactly what he was going
to do with the box.*

He stood so still that not one of his muscles moved –
not a finger, not a toe, nothing.

WHAT AM I?

When Bert went to school on Monday morning he looked at the fish tank and saw five fish swimming about in there. Good. They were still alive.

Miss King didn't seem to notice him. The whole morning went by and she didn't smile at him once, or wink at him with one eye the way she often did.

Probably she still remembered Friday, he thought. How awful it would be if she didn't like him any more!

After lunch a wasp landed on their table and Geraldine Greer tried to zap it with her jotter. WHACK, WALLOP, THUMP.

Three times she had a go at flattening it, and each time she missed. The wasp escaped towards the window pane.

"You leave that wasp alone," Bert told her.

"No."

"You will, I am the Friend of the Wasps," said Bert.

"If it comes near me again I am going to zap its brains in," cried Geraldine.

Luckily, Miss King told them all to tidy up, because they were going to play the WHAT AM I? game. This was good fun. You had to pretend to be something and the rest of the class had to guess what you were pretending to be. Bert shot his hand into the air, for he had a wonderful idea to keep the class guessing for ages and ages. However, Miss King chose Tommy Scott to be first.

The game began. Tommy marched to the front and got down on all-fours. Then he began to bark. Anyone could see that he was supposed to be a dog.

That was far too easy, thought Bert!

Now it was a girl's turn. Florence Courtney came to the front and stood there silently opening and closing her mouth until Meg guessed that she was a goldfish.

My idea is far better than that, thought Bert.

But it was Charlie's turn next. He lowered his head and suddenly refused to go to the front of the class.

"He's too shy!" Geraldine Greer piped up.

"Geraldine, put your bottom on that seat, please. Never mind, Charlie," said Miss King nicely, "perhaps next time. What about you, Bert – could you pretend to be something and keep us thinking for a long, long time?"

He certainly could!

Bert marched to the front of the classroom, where he threw off the new jumper that Liz had bought for him, and removed his socks and shoes. Tommy Scott stared at Bert's bare toes as if these were the first toes he had ever seen.

"Right. I'm starting."

Bert stuck out his head, and stretched out his arms, and poked out his fingers, and stood absolutely still. He stood so still that not one of his muscles moved – not a finger, not a toe, nothing.

I mustn't blink, he thought grimly.

"Goodness me!" said Miss King. "What on earth have we here?"

The room was quiet. Chairs creaked as the people in them thought as hard as they could think. They'll never guess, I have them fooled! thought Bert. In the silence it was also possible to hear that wasp buzzing.

Then the shrieking began. "Aaaa! It's on me. Get it off, get it off."

This was Geraldine Greer in a panic. Bert allowed his eyes to look sideways in time to see her jumping around and flailing her arms.

"Geraldine don't be so silly, the wasp isn't even near you," said Miss King.

The wasp went away, and the class settled down to watch Bert once more, who hadn't so much as twitched in all the commotion.

But the wasp found Bert at the front of the room – he saw it coming, he watched it buzz in circles round his nose and STILL he refused to move. When it landed on his bare arm, Meg just couldn't look.

"There's a wasp on you, Bert!" she cried.

There was, but he wasn't moving, wasp or no wasp – not until they guessed what he was supposed to be. Up his arm it crawled, tickling all the way.

"Miss!" Charlie's hand went up just as the wasp flew away. "He's a tailor's dummy, Miss King, I've seen them in shop windows."

At last Bert was able to drop his arms, and stretch his toes, and rub his itchy nose. As he put on his right sock he thought how you couldn't fool Charlie for ever.

"Indeed he is!" said Miss King. "And the best tailor's dummy I've ever seen. Did you all notice how he didn't even move when the wasp landed on his arm?"

"Did you see how my fingers were all pointy, Miss King?"

"Yes! And your bare toes. You are certainly the part, Bert Green, and I think you should feed the fish today before you go home!"

"By myself?"

"All on your own."

Bert glowed with pleasure and with pride. He gave the fish quite a lot of food in case they were feeling hungry after the weekend.

*"Everybody thinks I am your
mummy!"* Liz whispered.

Bert's New Mummy

Bert's daddy worked every day until half-past five, so Bert couldn't go home to his own house after school. He went to his Granny Green's instead and sometimes she was cross with him.

Granny Green didn't allow Bert to play in the street in case a car knocked him down. She didn't allow him to play in the Good Room where she had lovely ornaments, and he couldn't play upstairs in Granny Green's house because there was no upstairs. She lived in a bungalow.

On Tuesday Granny Green played hide-and-seek with Bert and she couldn't find him anywhere.

At last she gave up looking and called out loud: "Bert Green where are you? I hope you're not hiding in the Good Room or there'll be trouble."

"Boo!" shouted Bert, jumping out of the big grandfather clock in the hall. It had been a great hiding-place, but Granny Green didn't think so.

"Now look what you've done," she said. "That clock never stops and now it's not ticking any more. You'll have to behave yourself, my boy, when your daddy gets a stepmother for you. She won't want to live with a bad rascal."

A stepmother? What was that, Bert wondered. He'd never heard of such a thing.

His granny had plenty more clocks all over the place, and Bert was glad when their hands showed half-past five. Soon he heard the car arriving at the front door.

Bert ran outside, dumped his schoolbag in the back and jumped in after it. Liz was in the car, too.

"Hiya Bert," she said, "I'm coming over to your house for tea and I'm warning you, I'm starving, so you'd better have plenty of food."

Goody, thought Bert. He liked Liz to be in his house.

His daddy said, "I hope you were a good boy for your Granny Green."

"I was quite good," said Bert, deciding not to mention that he had stopped the big clock.

Next morning, when Bert went to school with his friends Charlie and Meg, he told them some important news. "My daddy might be getting a stepmother for me."

"What sort of a mother is a stepmother?" said Charlie.

Bert didn't answer, but Meg knew a lot about stepmothers. She had read about them in stories. "They can be wicked you know. Snow White had one who gave her poison in an apple and she was horrible. And Cinderella's stepmother made her do all the work in the kitchen. She got soot on her clothes because her stepmother didn't love her."

Bert, who was not happy with this kind of talk, decided that he didn't want a stepmother after all.

After school Bert and Meg and Charlie came down the path together.

"I see my mummy," said Meg.

Charlie said, "I see mine."

Bert had a lovely surprise. "I see Liz," he shouted, "she's waiting for me!"

Liz took Bert by the hand and they walked into town together. They went into the barber shop because Bert's hair was too long and he needed a haircut. He could see what was happening in the mirror. Every time the barber did snip-snip-snip with his scissors pieces of Bert's hair fell everywhere and his head seemed to grow smaller.

The barber said to Liz, "Your little boy is very like you."

"Do you really think so?"

"I do. That child's your double!"

Liz whispered into Bert's ear, "Did you hear that? The barber thinks I'm your mummy!"

I wish you were, thought Bert.

Next they went into the supermarket to buy some food. They bought a cauliflower and quite a lot of fruit. When the tomatoes needed weighing on the machine, Bert weighed them. By the time he had chosen some packets of biscuits for his school break, the trolley was half full.

"Can I push it?" asked Bert.

"Well all right, but be careful where you go," said Liz, "and push it gently."

So Bert began to push the trolley down the long shop. After a while he forgot that he was pushing a trolley. "Vroomvroom," he said to himself, gathering speed like a lorry driver, "vroom."

His trolley bashed into another one and almost turned it right over.

"Will you watch where you're going!" said an angry voice. "Look at my groceries on the floor."

"I am terribly sorry," said Liz.

"I should think so, one isn't even safe in a supermarket! Please keep your boy under control."

As Liz helped the lady to pick up the groceries, she whispered in Bert's ear: "That woman thinks you're my Bert. Everybody thinks I'm your mummy!"

I wish you were, thought Bert.

Now Liz and Bert went into a fishmonger's to buy six silver fish for tea. The fishmonger wrapped up the fish and handed them to Bert.

"Here you are, boyo, six fresh herrings. You carry those home for your mum."

Bert took the parcel and smiled up at Liz. Even the man who sold fish thought she was his mummy.

When Bert's daddy came home that evening he hugged Bert and gave Liz a kiss and then they had tea. His daddy ate three herrings, Liz ate two and Bert had one. He didn't like his fish much because it had too many small bones.

"Daddy," said Bert, "if you get me a stepmother will she be bad and make me do all the work?"

His daddy stopped eating. Then he stared at Bert with big eyes because he was so amazed. "Who said anything about a stepmother?"

"Granny Green. Meg knows all about them, she says they're horrible and I don't want one."

His daddy shook his head, then let out one of his big laughs "What about Liz – is she horrible?"

"No!" cried Bert. Liz wasn't horrible, she was one of his best people.

"Well that's good news, because Liz and I are getting married and she'll be coming to live in this house – here! – with you and me."

Now it was Bert's turn to be amazed. "All the time?"

"All the time."

Liz said, "We can do the work together,

Bert, if you like. I can meet you after school some days."

"You'll be able to tuck him into bed at night," his daddy said.

"Of course I'll tuck him in."

"I think you'll have to tell him stories."

"Oh, there'll be stories. I know lots of stories," smiled Liz.

Bert was happy. This was wonderful News. He gobbled the rest of his tea, gave Liz a big hug, and ran out to find Charlie and Meg. He wanted to tell those two about his nice new mummy.

THE

END

MORE WALKER STORY BOOKS
For You to Enjoy

☐ 0-7445-5482-9   *In Crack Willow Wood*
by Sam McBratney / Ivan Bates   £3.50

☐ 0-7445-5456-X   *The Kit Stories*
by Jane Gardam / Paul Howard   £3.50

☐ 0-7445-4381-9   *One For Me, One For You*
by Rita Phillips Mitchell /
Paul Howard   £3.50

☐ 0-7445-6084-5   *Willa and Old Miss Annie*
by Berlie Doherty / Kim Lewis   £3.50

☐ 0-7445-6024-1   *Fiona Says...*
by Diana Hendry /
Dave McTaggart   £3.50

☐ 0-7445-6036-5   *The Owl and Billy Stories*
by Martin Waddell /
Priscilla Lamont   £3.50

☐ 0-7445-3089-X   *Here Comes Tod*
by Philippa Pearce / Adriano Gon   £3.50

Name _____

Address _____

_____